JUV

Mason, Jane

Star Wars Revenge of the
Sith -Obi-Wan's Foe

AR Pts. 0.5
BL 4.8

A NOTE TO PARENTS

When your children are ready to "step into reading," giving them the right books is as crucial to their development as giving them the right food to eat. **Star Wars®** **Jedi Readers** feature exciting stories and information reinforced with lively, colorful illustrations that make learning to read fun, satisfying, and rewarding.

Learning to read, Step by Step:

- **Step 1** books (Preschool–Grade 1) have easy-to-read type, short sentences, and simple stories.
- **Step 2** books (Grades 1–3) offer longer and slightly more difficult text while introducing contractions and clauses.
- **Step 3** books (Grades 2–3) present paragraphs, chapters, and fully developed plotlines in fiction and nonfiction.
- **Step 4** books (Grades 2–4) feature thrilling fiction and nonfiction with exciting illustrations for independent as well as reluctant readers.

Remember: The grade levels assigned to the steps are intended only as guides. Some children move through all the steps rapidly; others climb the steps over a period of a few years. Either way, these books will help children "step into reading" for life!

To Lucy, with heartfelt thanks for introducing us
—Jane and Sarah

This one's for Scarlett . . .
my intergalactic princess
—Tommy Lee

www.randomhouse.com/kids
www.starwars.com

Library of Congress Cataloging-in-Publication Data
Mason, Jane B.
Obi-Wan's foe / by Jane Mason & Sarah Stephens ; illustrated by Tommy Lee Edwards.
    p.   cm. — (Jedi readers. A step 4 book.)
"Star wars."
SUMMARY: During the Clone Wars, Obi-Wan Kenobi confronts General Grievous, supreme commander of the droid armies.
ISBN 0-375-82609-2 (trade) — ISBN 0-375-92609-7 (lib. bdg.)
[1. Science fiction.] I. Stephens, Sarah. II. Edwards, Tommy Lee, ill.
III. Title. IV. Series: Jedi readers. Step 4 book.
PZ7.M4116Ob 2005 [Fic]—dc22 2004018901

Printed in the United States of America First Edition 10 9 8 7 6 5 4 3 2 1

JEDI READERS

STAR WARS®

REVENGE OF THE SITH™
OBI-WAN'S FOE

BY JANE MASON AND SARAH STEPHENS
ILLUSTRATED BY TOMMY LEE EDWARDS

A Step 4 Book

Random House New York

1
SPECIAL SESSION

Obi-Wan Kenobi and Anakin Skywalker sat
in the Council Chamber with several other
Jedi. Master Mace Windu had called a
special session.

These special meetings were becoming
more and more common. War was raging.
The Jedi were the guardians of the
threatened Republic.

But Obi-Wan sensed something different about this session. Could it be a turning point? Were they on the brink of something big? He hoped so.

The war seemed never-ending. The Jedi and their clone army fought against the Separatists and their droid armies. But the Separatists had more than droids on their side. They had the evil Sith Lord Count Dooku and his henchman, General Grievous.

"General Grievous has been located," Mace announced. "He is on the planet Utapau."

Obi-Wan suppressed a shudder. General Grievous was the supreme commander of the droid armies. Long ago, Grievous had been a general on his homeworld, Kalee. Then he was almost killed in a shuttle crash.

The Sith had been watching Grievous. They needed a leader for their droids. They kept him alive. They hired Geonosian cyborg experts to combine his living parts with a hard ceramic shell. And that was not all.

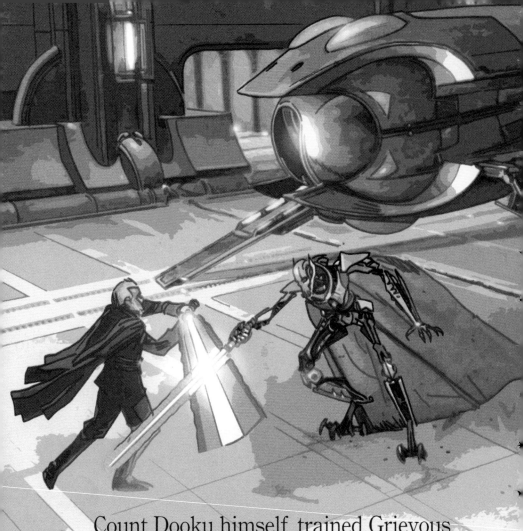

Count Dooku himself trained Grievous
to fight with a lightsaber. With his cyborg
body and Sith training, Grievous had
become a dangerous enemy to the Jedi.

"We have received no reports about
Grievous from our agents on Utapau,"
Ki-Adi-Mundi said. The Jedi with the tall,
pointed head looked troubled.

"A partial message was intercepted in a diplomatic packet," Anakin said. "It was from the leader of Utapau."

Yoda spoke quietly but firmly. "Act on this, we must." He tapped his gimer stick on the ground for emphasis.

All of the Jedi on the Council agreed.

Obi-Wan noticed that Anakin sat up a bit straighter. "The Chancellor has requested that I lead the campaign," Anakin announced.

The Council Chamber was silent. The other Jedi were clearly troubled.

Mace Windu's eyes revealed his annoyance. "The Council will decide who is to go, not the Chancellor."

Anakin just stared at the floor.

Obi-Wan knew the Council was right. The Jedi were defenders of the Republic, but they did not take orders from any one leader. And Chancellor Palpatine was proving harder and harder to trust. Obi-Wan wanted to talk to Anakin alone and help him understand.

"A Master is needed—a Jedi with more experience," Yoda said.

"Our resources are limited," Mace added. "I recommend we send only one Jedi . . . Master Kenobi."

2
HOSTAGES

Obi-Wan stood next to his purple and gray Jedi fighter in the Republic battle cruiser hangar. Several clone commanders were lined up before him.

"Most of the cities on Utapau are on one small continent. We should be able to land undetected if we approach from the far side," said Clone Commander Cody.

"I'll keep them distracted until you arrive," Obi-Wan said. "But don't take too long."

Obi-Wan felt confident climbing into his Jedi fighter. The last time Obi-Wan had battled Grievous, the general had fled in an escape pod. But this time Obi-Wan had two clone trooper brigades to help him. Commander Cody would not let him down.

Soon Obi-Wan was skimming over the surface of Utapau. The green planet appeared featureless at first. Then Obi-Wan noticed a few small rock spires and something else—enormous sinkholes bored deep into the planet. These giant holes were so big that they housed entire cities.

Obi-Wan landed skillfully on a platform inside one of the giant sinkholes. A local administrator named Tion Medon met Obi-Wan as he stepped out of his ship.

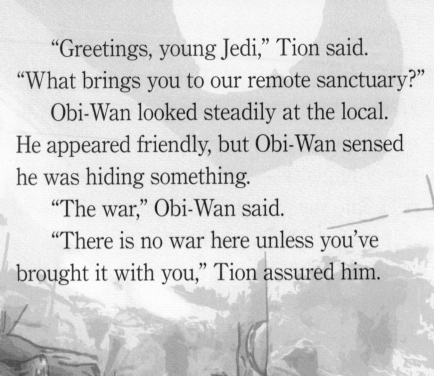

"Greetings, young Jedi," Tion said.
"What brings you to our remote sanctuary?"

Obi-Wan looked steadily at the local.
He appeared friendly, but Obi-Wan sensed
he was hiding something.

"The war," Obi-Wan said.

"There is no war here unless you've
brought it with you," Tion assured him.

Soon Obi-Wan was skimming over the surface of Utapau. The green planet appeared featureless at first. Then Obi-Wan noticed a few small rock spires and something else—enormous sinkholes bored deep into the planet. These giant holes were so big that they housed entire cities.

Obi-Wan landed skillfully on a platform inside one of the giant sinkholes. A local administrator named Tion Medon met Obi-Wan as he stepped out of his ship.

"Greetings, young Jedi," Tion said. "What brings you to our remote sanctuary?"

Obi-Wan looked steadily at the local. He appeared friendly, but Obi-Wan sensed he was hiding something.

"The war," Obi-Wan said.

"There is no war here unless you've brought it with you," Tion assured him.

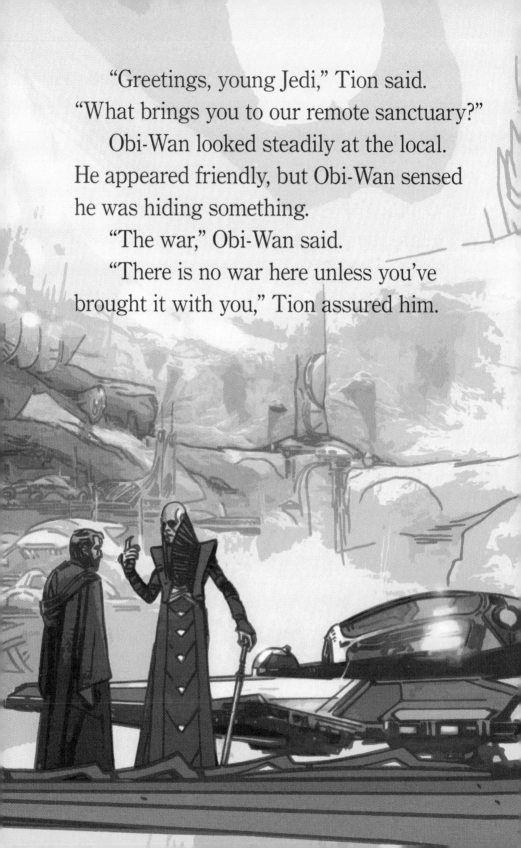

Obi-Wan's gaze did not falter. "With your kind permission, I'd like some fuel and to use your city as a base to search nearby systems."

Tion nodded and a ground crew rushed out to refuel Obi-Wan's fighter.

"What are you searching for?" Tion asked.

"A droid army, led by General Grievous," Obi-Wan said.

Tion leaned in close to Obi-Wan. "He is here!" he whispered. "We are being held hostage. They are watching us."

Obi-Wan nodded. His heart raced, but his face revealed nothing. His information and instincts had been correct. "I understand," he said.

"The tenth level," Tion confided. "Thousands of battle droids . . ."

"Have your people take shelter," Obi-Wan said quietly. "And if you have warriors, now is the time."

Obi-Wan had found his foe.

3
FINDING TRANSPORT

"What was his name?" General Grievous's droid bodyguard demanded. He stood with Tion Medon on the Utapau observation deck.

The administrator shrugged. "He didn't say." Above them, the Jedi fighter zoomed into space. "I told you, all he wanted was fuel."

But in the landing platform hallway, Obi-Wan also watched his ship take off. The Jedi's astromech droid, R4-G9, flew the ship while Obi-Wan stayed hidden on the ground. He quietly moved up a stairway cut into the side of the sinkhole.

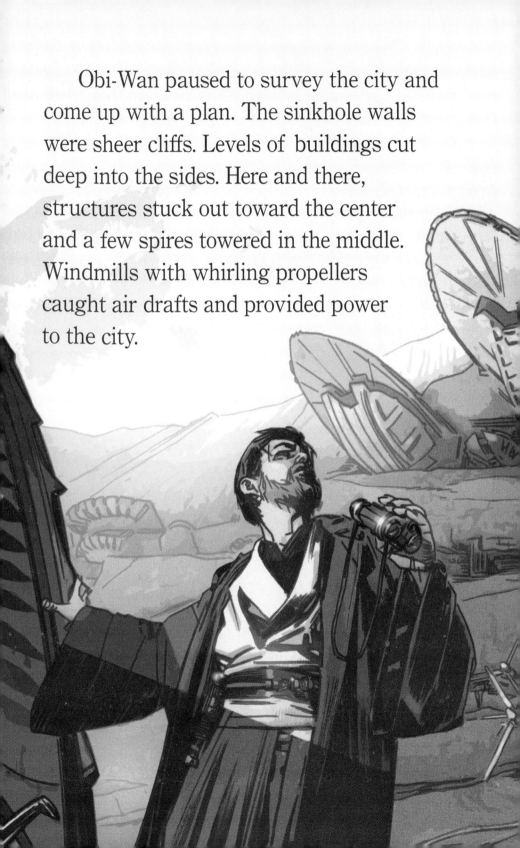

Obi-Wan paused to survey the city and come up with a plan. The sinkhole walls were sheer cliffs. Levels of buildings cut deep into the sides. Here and there, structures stuck out toward the center and a few spires towered in the middle. Windmills with whirling propellers caught air drafts and provided power to the city.

Obi-Wan looked at the tenth level with his electrobinoculars. It was several hundred meters above him. He needed a fast way up.

A strange, bellowing cry interrupted Obi-Wan's thoughts. He followed the sound to a corral filled with a dozen dragon-like lizards and their wranglers. The beasts of burden were perfectly suited to travel on Utapau. They could scale walls with their sticky reptilian feet.

Obi-Wan walked up to one of the wranglers. He waved his hand slightly and began to speak. He was using the Force.

"I need transportation," he said.

The wrangler watched Obi-Wan's hand as if in a daze. "You need transportation," he repeated.

"Get it for me," Obi-Wan said.

"I will get it for you," the wrangler replied. He turned to the other wranglers and began talking in his native tongue.

Obi-Wan walked along the line of dragon-lizards. He examined each one carefully, looking into its catlike eyes. Then he made his decision.

"This one," he told the wrangler.

The wrangler untied the lizard. "Boga. She answers to Boga," he said.

Obi-Wan swung himself easily onto Boga's back. The lizard reared up and scurried to the edge of the sinkhole. The Jedi patted the lizard on the neck. "Good girl, Boga," he said. Obi-Wan wasn't used to working alone. It felt good to be part of a team again.

4
BATTLING THE BODYGUARDS

Obi-Wan guided Boga straight up the wall
of the sinkhole past buildings and balconies.
Finally they reached the tenth level. The Jedi
and Boga stepped into the middle of the
huge Separatist control center.

General Grievous towered at the far end
of the room. His skull-like faceplate
protected evil eyes. His long arms ended in
mechanical claws. He looked strong enough
to crush anything in his path.

"General Kenobi," Grievous said. "You
are a bold one. But I find your behavior
bewildering. Surely you realize you are
doomed."

A hundred battle droids made a circle
around Obi-Wan, General Grievous, and his
robot bodyguards.

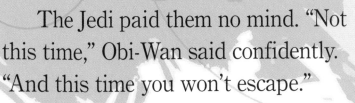

The Jedi paid them no mind. "Not this time," Obi-Wan said confidently. "And this time you won't escape."

The bodyguards swung their electrostaffs. The Jedi ducked, allowing the staffs to whistle over his head. Before the guards could react, Obi-Wan ignited his lightsaber and cut one of them in half.

The battle had begun.

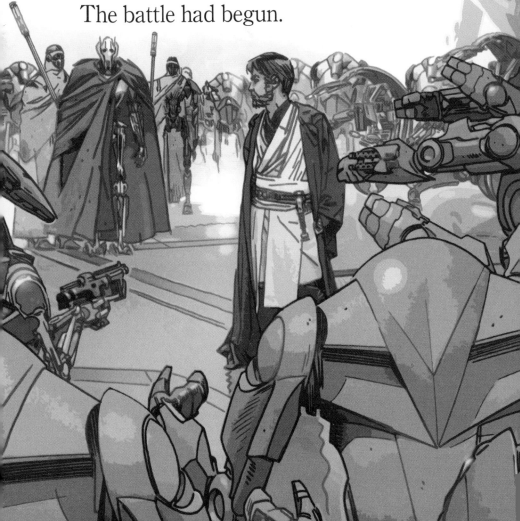

As the bodyguard fell to the ground in a heap, Grievous caught its electrostaff. The three remaining bodyguards wasted no time. They lunged at Obi-Wan.

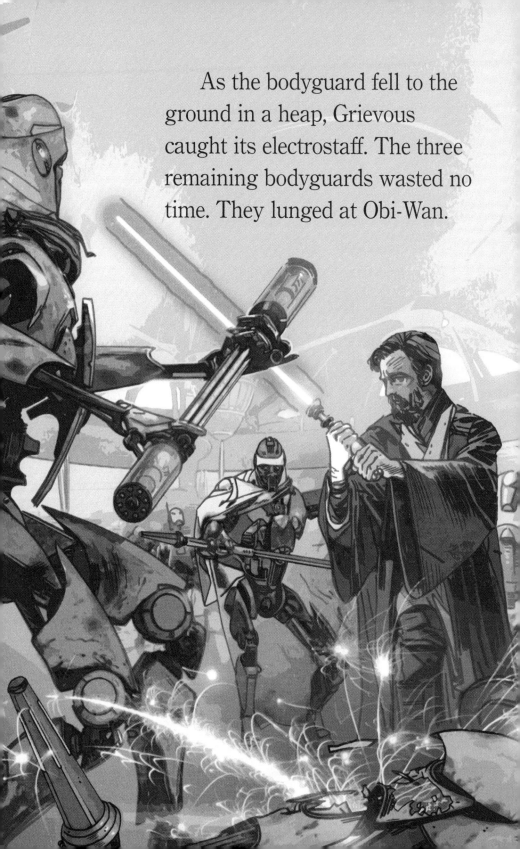

All around them, battle droids kept their weapons trained on the Jedi and the bodyguards. Grievous was motionless. Still holding the electrostaff, he watched the battle between Obi-Wan and his three guards closely.

Electrostaffs and lightsaber sliced through the air with fury. Obi-Wan leaped lightly away from the deadly staffs as the bodyguards tracked him across the room. He used the Force to anticipate the guards' next moves and evade them. More than once, a spectator battle droid was cut down in the fight.

At last Obi-Wan broke away. The bodyguards gave chase, their staffs hissing in the air. Then Obi-Wan sliced through a metal strut that was holding up a large cargo container. With a loud crunch, the container fell and crushed the three remaining guards.

5
OUTNUMBERED

"Blast him!" Grievous commanded furiously.

The battle droids surrounding Obi-Wan
fired their weapons. Laser bolts rained all
around the lone Jedi.

Jumping into the air, Obi-Wan grabbed
a cable hanging from the ceiling. The odds
were against him, but the Force was all
around. He called on it as he swung upward,
deflecting a barrage of laser bolts with his
lightsaber. A moment later, he disappeared
into a tangled mass of equipment hanging
just below the ceiling.

KA-BOOM! The droids fired so many
laser bolts into the equipment that they
caused a huge explosion. Flaming pieces of
metal crashed to the floor.

Obi-Wan gracefully leaped down along
with the fiery metal.

Igniting his lightsaber, he cut down
several more battle droids.

When the smoke finally cleared,
Obi-Wan found himself face to face with
General Grievous. It was the moment he had
been waiting for.

"Attack, Kenobi," Grievous said. "I have
been trained in your Jedi arts by Count
Dooku himself."

Obi-Wan knew he should not take the
general's skills lightly. Grievous had killed
more Jedi than anyone else. Still, Obi-Wan
did not feel afraid.

Suddenly the general's mechanical arms each divided in two. All at once he pulled four lightsabers from his belt. Obi-Wan recognized with sadness that these lightsabers had once belonged to his fellow Jedi Knights. With effort, Obi-Wan cleared his mind. He focused on the task at hand. Revenge is not the Jedi way. Obi-Wan needed to win this battle for the good of the Republic.

Grievous sprang into action with four flashing lightsabers. The two fighters whirled in a deadly display of swordsmanship. Obi-Wan wielded his weapon with strength and grace. It was barely enough. He scrambled to defend himself against the attack. Desperately deflecting the flashing lightsabers, he crossed the control room. On every side, the remaining battle droids fired at him.

Obi-Wan was in trouble.

6
FIGHTING BACK

Obi-Wan gathered his strength. He would
not give up. Grievous was a terrible foe, but
the Force was stronger. Obi-Wan called on it.

He wielded his lightsaber with incredible speed, knocking Grievous's blades to the ground. First one, then another. Then another and another, until all four of the cyborg's weapons were gone.

It seemed like Obi-Wan was going to win the fight when the droids fired more laser bolts into the air. Grievous disappeared in the smoky battle. Obi-Wan fell down. His lightsaber skittered across the floor and stopped in front of a super battle droid.

"Careful with that," a battle droid warned as the super battle droid picked it up. "It's a lightsaber."

The super battle droid inspected the weapon. "A what?" he asked.

He did not have time to hear the answer. He ignited the lightsaber by mistake and cut off his own head!

"Hold your fire!" Grievous's voice suddenly echoed in the smoke-filled chamber.

Obi-Wan was nowhere to be seen.

"What are you trying to accomplish, Kenobi?" Grievous shouted. "I have thousands of troops. You will not defeat them."

Out of nowhere, Obi-Wan jumped into the air and reached for his lightsaber. It flew toward him and landed firmly in his hand. A split second later, the Jedi landed on top of a control station.

"I may not defeat your droids, but my troops certainly will," Obi-Wan said.

"Your troops will never penetrate my defenses," Grievous replied.

"Don't count on it," Obi-Wan said.

7
HEATING UP

An explosion echoed through the sinkhole.
Grievous and Obi-Wan both looked toward
the command center entrance. Outside, clone
troopers fiercely attacked battle droids. On
the far wall of the sinkhole, more clone
troopers rappelled onto balconies.

Dozens of clone troopers descended into
the entrance of the control center. They
blasted their weapons at the droids. The
room was instantly filled with flying laser
bolts, debris, and smoke.

The troops had arrived. Obi-Wan could focus his attack on Grievous instead of battling droids. He attacked again. Grievous fought back with an electrostaff. The two matched each other blow for blow. The general was too strong. Obi-Wan knew he needed to find a weakness to gain the upper hand.

A blast from a super battle droid distracted Obi-Wan momentarily. It was all the general needed. Obi-Wan did not sense Grievous's next move until it was too late. The general delivered a swift blow that sent the Jedi skidding across the floor.

General Grievous jumped onto his wheel bike and fled. Obi-Wan jumped to his feet. The general would not get away this time. Obi-Wan was determined. Swiftly he mounted Boga and gave chase.

Moving quickly down the wall of the sinkhole, Obi-Wan spotted Grievous ahead of them. Grievous spun his wheel bike around and took off in another direction. Obi-Wan and Boga were hot on his heels.

All around, droids and clones battled. Some of the people of Utapau fought with the clones against the droids. Others hid in whatever shelter they could find.

Obi-Wan and General Grievous hurtled through the city at breakneck speed. They passed battle zones, exploding buildings, and troops of all kinds.

Boga panted as she tried to keep up with Grievous's wheel bike. Obi-Wan knew how she felt. He was tiring, too, but he urged the big lizard on.

"You can do it, girl," he said.

Grievous led Obi-Wan to an area covered with the giant windmills the Jedi had seen when he landed. The windmill blades were enormous. They were still, but not for long. From the other side of a windmill, Grievous released the brakes on one of the giant propellers. The huge blades began to spin with deadly speed. They made a lethal barrier.

Boga stopped short. General Grievous was out of reach.

Laughing evilly, Grievous switched on his comlink.

"Prepare to move out of orbit," he said to his command ship above. "I will be up in a few moments."

8

THE CHASE CONTINUES

Obi-Wan took a moment to size up the situation. He had to get to Grievous—and quickly. He gently coaxed his reptilian steed closer to the deadly blades. Then he ignited his lightsaber and forced it into the whirling windmill. Pieces of metal blade flew in all directions. Obi-Wan barely avoided being hit.

Several meters away, Grievous accelerated over a huge gap. He activated the claws of his wheel bike. A moment later, the bike's strong legs and claws clung to a second set of windmill blades.

Obi-Wan urged Boga forward, and the lizard leaped across the gaping hole. They barely made it to the other side. General Grievous was already racing ahead.

Obi-Wan followed Grievous into the Utapau tunnel system. Zooming up the tunnel walls in his wheel bike, Grievous easily avoided the oncoming traffic. Boga used her lizard feet to cling to the tunnel ceiling. Obi-Wan closed the distance between them.

Trusting in Boga and the Force, Obi-Wan reached out and grabbed the general's electrostaff. Locked together, Obi-Wan and Grievous raced out of the tunnel onto a secret landing platform. A Trade Federation fighter sat in the middle of it.

Yanking on the staff, Obi-Wan jumped from Boga's back to the general's wheel bike. They were both knocked to the ground.

Grievous pulled out a blaster pistol and fired. Obi-Wan deflected the bolts with Grievous's own electrostaff. The Jedi felt his energy return. The battle had gone on long enough.

Obi-Wan charged, swinging the electrostaff and hitting the half-machine in the stomach. Grievous's blaster pistol slid across the floor. Obi-Wan struck again, this time bending the general's arm.

Grievous was furious! He grabbed Obi-Wan and knocked away the electrostaff. It was down to hand-to-hand combat—cyborg versus Jedi.

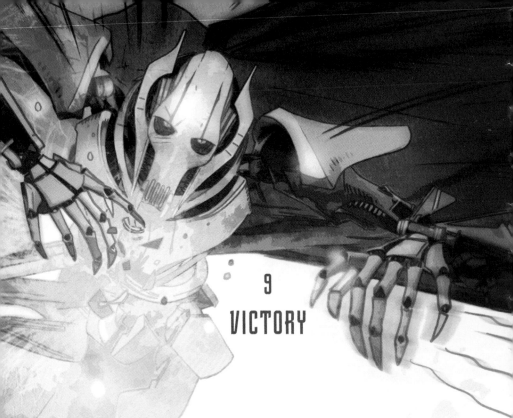

9
VICTORY

Obi-Wan used every ounce of concentration
to avoid the general's deadly blows. Grievous
was powerful. His machine parts and Sith
training made him seem unstoppable. Obi-
Wan leaped, ducked, and dove to avoid being
killed. He was tired, but he believed in the
Force. He waited for his opportunity.

At last Obi-Wan spotted a weakness in
the general's defenses. His stomach plate had
been knocked loose!

Obi-Wan did not waste a second. He grabbed the plate, pulling it off completely. Now the cyborg's alien guts were visible. Apart from the eyes, the only living part of the horrible general was in a bag inside his metal chest.

Grievous's arm seized Obi-Wan, lifted him into the air, and tossed him across the landing platform. Then he charged!

A split second before Grievous was upon him, Obi-Wan extended his hand. He used the Force to call the general's blaster pistol to him. Several laser bolts hit Grievous in the belly. The general exploded from the inside out. What remained of the smoldering cyborg fell to the ground.

Relief washed over Obi-Wan. He had completed his mission. The evil Grievous had been stopped for good. Obi-Wan looked forward to sharing the news with Anakin and the Jedi Council. The end of General Grievous was a big step toward peace.